Books by

The Intellectual Rebel
Aphorisms
Speculative Aphorisms
Speculative Aphorisms II
Philoscience
Philoscience II
Intellectual Jazz
Intellectual Jazz II
Jazzism
Neoliberal Arts
Neoliberal Arts II
Postmodern Minimalist Philosophy
Simpletism
Uncertaintyism
The Ultimate Truth
Anything Is Possible
Political and Social Observations
The University of Neoliberal Arts
A New Breed of Philosophers
Ferreirism - The Ultimate Philosophy
The eChurch of Zerotropy
The Ferreira Genesis Equation
Zerotropism and Panaceanism
Philosophy Should Belong to the Masses

Please visit my website at:
http://www.philophysics.com

Thank You!

Programming the World with Philosophy

By Keith N. Ferreira

iUniverse, Inc.
New York   Bloomington

Programming the World with Philosophy

Copyright © 2009 by Keith N. Ferreira

iUniverse books may be ordered through booksellers or by contacting:

iUniverse
1663 Liberty Drive
Bloomington, IN 47403
www.iuniverse.com
1-800-Authors (1-800-288-4677)

ISBN: 978-1-4401-6284-8 (pbk)
ISBN: 978-1-4401-6285-5 (ebk)

Printed in the United States of America

iUniverse rev. date: 9/10/2009

Table of Contents

Programming the World with Philosophy (Part One) 1
 Programming the World with Philosophy 1
 Spiritual Gods Might Be a Dime a Dozen 1
 The Rat-Race Model of Education Can Only Produce
 Rats 2
 In a Rat-Race Economic System 2
 Schrodinger's Cat Paradox 3
 Brane Theory 3
 The Ultimate Jazzon Theory 4
 The Ultimate Physical Reductionist Theory 4
 A Jazzon Is a Point Particle 5
 Pragmamaterialism 5
 Scientists Have Discovered God 6
 Hell and Damnation vs Healing the Sick 6
 Quantum Entanglement Computer Research 7
 The Ultimate Truth about Religion 7
 The Mental Jazzon 8
 Algorithms and Complexity 8
 Where Is the Evidence that Entropy is Increasing in the
 Universe? 9
 President-Elect Barack Obama Fulfills My Prophecy 9
 I Would Like Professionals to Do Me One Favor 10
 Philosophy Is the Key to Educating the Masses 10
 Philosophy Is the Ultimate Substitute for Religion 11
 Repossession of Property Is Almost Always a Bad Idea 11
 The Ultimate Algorithm 12
 The Minds of Nonzero Entropy Entities 12
 The Mind Is the Reciprocal of God 13
 Even If One Does not Study Any of My Writings 13
 My Writings Can Educate One to an Unprecedented
 Level 14
 A Very Deep Question 14
 Philosophy Vindicates the Thoughts of Everyone 15
 Philosophy Can Prove Anything 15

A Nonelitist Education for the Masses 16
My Philosophy of Education 16
Four Questions for Religious Conservatives 17
Philosophy: The Ultimate Opium of the Masses 17
Telepathic Sex, Etc. 18
Language Is Potentially an Infinite Source of Enlightenment 18
Philosophy Vindicates Religion 19
Judeo-Christian Ethics Are Flawed 19
Stating that Philosophy Can Prove Anything Does not Invalidate Philosophy 20
The World Democratic Revolution Is Alive and Well 20
The World Grassroots Democratic Revolution 21
Anthropicism 21
Laissez-Faire Capitalism Is Dead 22
The Problem of Government Red Tape 22
Western Science, Technology, and Philosophy Are Dead 23
The Myth of Scientific Knowledge and Wisdom 23
The Myth of Religious Knowledge and Wisdom 24
The Myth of Philosophical Knowledge and Wisdom 24
The Myth of Knowledge and Wisdom in General 25
Knowledge and Wisdom Are Dead 25
Programming the World with Philosophy (Part Two) 26
Descartes: "I Think, Therefore I Am" Is Dead 26
The Death of Western Thought Is at Hand 26
From Now On 27
High-Energy Particle Physics Is no Longer Relevant 27
The New Heart of Mainstream Scientific Research 28
Postmodern Neoclassical Educators 28
The Educationally Crippled and Abandoned Masses 29
The Concept of a Unified Theory of Entropy 29
I Want the Masses to Know 30
I Am Surprised 30
Zero Entropy Is Spiritual in Nature 31
The True Nature of Spirituality 31

Scientists Insinuate About the Implications of Zero
Entropy   32
Religious Creationists Have a Foolproof Argument   32
The Zero-Entropy Argument for the Existence of God   33
My Writings Should not Be Taken as Gospel   33
Modern Technology Is Dead   34
Intellectual Activity Is Dead   34
Human Languages and Feynman Diagrams   35
Infinite Regresses Are not Impossible in Nature   35
There Are Infinities in Nature   36
A Tree Is Known by the Fruits It Bears   36
Postmodern Minimalist Civilization   37
The Meaning of the Name: William Shakespeare   37
A Crappy Philosophy   38
Dominating Mainstream Scientific Research   38
The Endgame of Science, Technology, and Philosophy   39
Romulus and Remus   39
Africa and Postmodern Minimalist Science and
Technology   40
The End of Science and Technology Is in Sight   40
Africa: The Dark Horse of International Politics   41
Latin America and the Caribbean   41
All the Nations of the World   42
An Invitation to Teachers and Professors Around the
World   42
The Masses Educated Can Never Be Defeated   43
In My Opinion, Yahoo! Is the Best Search Engine on the
Internet   43
An Experiment for Psychologists to Perform   44
In Every Economic Downturn   44
The Postmodern Minimalist Way of Worshipping God   45
Entropy and Conscious Sophistication   45
Western Philosophy Is Dead   46
Western Philosophy Is the Apex of a University
Education   46
The Concept of the Characteristics of Zero   47

Only One of an Infinite Number of Realities 47
Zero Entropy in Our Reality Might not Be Fundamental 48
Mental Illness and Perceptions 48
Our Reality Consists of One Jazzon 49
Religion Is Dead 49
God Is Now in the Domain of Science 50
Everything Is Dead 50
Programming the World with Philosophy (Part Three) 51
My Definition of the Aphorism 51
If Anyone Has a Better Plan for Educating the Masses 51
What Is the Alternative to Neoliberal Arts 52
Even If 52
The Ultimate Reductionist and Antireductionist
Concepts 53
It's All an Illusion 53
God Is an Illusory Characteristic of Zero 54
Zeroisticism 54
What Is the Answer? 55
In the Beginning Was Chaos 55
I Am Surprised and Disappointed 56
Chaos Is Another Name for Entropy 56
Professionals Will Find My Websites Very Informative 57
Perhaps, I Am Just a Crazy Fool 57
Zero Is the Answer to All Questions 58
The Ultimate Minimalist Education 58
If the Masses Were to Learn Zero from My Websites 59
The Brahmans of India Were Correct After All 59
I Have Succeeded in Educating the Masses of the
World 60
Neoliberal Arts and the New World Order 60
The Nature of the Mind 61
Hedonism and the Future of Humanity 61
Infinity Is a Number 62
All Numbers Are Undefined 62
I Do not See Why Zero Cannot Have Nonzero
Characteristics 63

Even If the Story of Jesus in the Bible Is True   63
Dangerous Cultural Atavists and Demagogues   64
Educultism   64
Anti-Educultism   65
The Quantum of Action Is the Gateway to Zero Entropy   65
The Ultimate Unified Theory of Nature   66
Beyond the Standard Model of Quantum Mechanics   66
Religious Asses Plain and Simple   67
Nonatavistic and Nonparochialistic   67
God's Message Should Undergo Paradigm Shifts   68
Zerotropism Is the New Religious Paradigm   68
Africa Can Still Come Out on Top Internationally   69
I Can Be Considered to Be a Postmodern Minimalist
Prophet   69
The Ultimate Paradigm Shift   70
The Most Difficult Concept in Nature to Grasp   70
Where My Websites Are Most Popular   71
Singularities Are Impossible in Nature   71
Difficult-to-Teach Students   72
C Students   72
America Is Beginning to Rediscover the Potential of Its
Creative C Students   73
"Home in Three Days. Don't Wash"   73
Conscious Perceptions   74
Perturbism   74
The Nature of Consciousness from the Physical
Perspective   75
The Nature of God from the Scientific Perspective   75
Programming the World with Philosophy (Part Four)   76
All Nerve Related Activity   76
I Have Often Wondered   76
Classical and Nonclassical Perturbism   77
Classical and Nonclassical Swarmism   78
My Websites Will Serve as Inspiration   78
Nonzero Entropy   79
Nikolai Fedorovich Fedorov's Dream Is Attainable   79

Original Philosophy Has an Endless Future 80
The Theory of Original Ideas 80
Proof that Original Philosophy Is Endless 81
A Zero Entropy State Is an Example of a Concrete
Infinity 81
The Only Way that Philosophy Can Proceed 82
Philosophy Will Never Die 82
Solipsism and the Human Mind 83
Entropy and the Scientific Enterprise 83
Creative C Students and World Domination 84
Fundamental Particle Physics Research Is Dead 84
The American Nietzsche for the Twenty-First Century 85
Sexual Orgasms and the Immune System Response 85
Sexual Orgasms and Orange Juice 86
Teaching the Masses How to Be Intellectually Creative 86
Creative C Students and Academia 87
The Creation Vs Evolution Debate Is Misguided 87
The True Purpose of Science and Technology 88
Neoliberal Arts as a Source of Inspiration 88
Postmodern Minimalist Religion 89
Philosophy Will Enable the Masses to Elevate Each
Other 89
Postmodern Minimalist Literature 90
The Masses Can Become Nobody's Fool 90
The Judeo-Christian Bible Proves Nothing Even If It Is
True 91
Beyond the Truth or Falsity of Any Religious Text 91
Philosophy Will Never, and Should Never Become a
Science 92
Keith N. Ferreira Is a Trinidad & Tobago Born American
philosopher 92
A World-Class Education for Each Member of the
Masses Is within Reach 93
PhD = Doctor of Philosophy 93
Science Proves Nothing Even If It Is True 94
Beyond the Truth or Falsity of Science 94

Philosophy Is Beyond Truth and Falsity   95
Academically Proficient Students   95
A Very Difficult Concept to Grasp   96
Insentience Is a Characteristic of Zero   96
Education Is a Form of Programming   97
Beyond Science, Technology, and Religion   97
The Masses Can Transcend Science, Technology, and
Religion   98
The Pseudo-Expansion of the Universe   98
Proof that the Universe Is not Expanding   99
The Pseudo Dark-Energy Problem   99
Zero and Infinity Have Zero Entropy   100
Proof that Everything Is in the Mind of God   100
The Dead Are Insentient Beings   101
Programming the World with Philosophy (Part Five)   102
Zero Is the Ultimate Fractal   102
An Important New Philosophical Concept   102
Nothingness and Nonexistence Are Characteristics of
Zero   103
Entropy Is the Devil, While Anti-Entropy Is the Messiah
103
Zero Consists of the Ferreira Fundamental Trinity   104
I Would Like to Motivate Blacks   104
A Part of Advanced Black Culture and Tradition   105
The World Political Endgame   105
Zero Entropy Is Relative   106
The Hindus Believe that God Is Ineffable   106
Japan   107
Undivine Intelligent Design   107
Philosophy Is Meant to Be Enjoyable Like Good Music 108
The Masses and My Writings   108
The Joys of Thinking for Oneself   109
An Education vs An Academic Degree   109
Science, Technology, and Religion Are Parochial
Enterprises   110
Neoliberal Arts vs Liberal Arts   110

When One Owes the Mafia a Debt 111
Proof that the Search for Truth Is Dead 111
Hedonism and Neoliberal Arts 112
The Ultimate Truth 112
Armageddon Is the Ultimate Entropic Orgy 113
Neoliberal Arts and the Quest to Conquer Entropy 113
Postmoderm Minimalist Civilization 114
Africa Can Leapfrog the Rest of the World 114
I Believe in Rooting for the Underdogs 115
Entropy and the Masses 115
Proof that the Masses Love Entropy 116
The Bible Could Be True 116
Apocalyptic Culture 117
Here Is a Deeply Depressing Thought 117
Ferreira's Paradoxes and the Mysteries of Nature 118
All Realities Are Generated by Computer Simulations 118
Simulativism 119
Subconscious Itches 119
Neoliberal Arts Is a Singular Noun 120
Simulativism Can Explain All Phenomena 120
The Simulativistic Theory of Everything (STOE) 121
Conscious Computers vs Fundamental Particles 121
Infinite Regresses Are Possible in Nature 122
Why Don't the Masses Like to Think for Themselves? 122
Education Diplomas = Work Permits 123
Academic Degrees = Work Permits 123
Humanity and Important New Original Ideas 124
A Comprehensive Mathematical Theory of Complexity
Is not Possible 124
Even If the God of the Bible Is True 125
Even if Armageddon Is True 125
Even if Heaven and Hell Are True 126
Even if Science and Technology Are True 126

Programming the World with Philosophy (Part One)

Programming the World with Philosophy

If one has philosophical talent, one can program the world with one's own philosophy over the Internet. The Internet is allowing ordinary people like you and me to have our opportunities to influence the whole world with our own philosophies. Please make use of this great opportunity now, because no one knows for sure what tomorrow will bring. Try and program the world for the better, and you might be surprised at how much fun it is. To me, trying to program the world for the better with my philosophical writings is more fun than gambling, sex, or drugs. It should be noted that the lists of courses taken by students each semester at colleges and universities are called programs. Believe it or not! QED! (10/30/08)

Spiritual Gods Might Be a Dime a Dozen

Creating spiritual Gods might be as easy as creating desktop computer realities in desktop nonclassical computers. Therefore, spiritual Gods who are the creators of human realities might be as common and insignificant as grains of sand on all the beaches that exist. In other words, spiritual Gods might be a dime a dozen, and so might divine creations be a dime a dozen also. (11/1/08)

Keith N. Ferreira

The Rat-Race Model of Education Can Only Produce Rats

Professionals are responsible for the state of the so-called "ignorant masses," because professionals make their disciplines unnecessarily difficult to understand by making the education process an excruciatingly difficult rat race in which only those with truly rat-like qualities can win. In other words, the rat-race model of education can only produce rats. Believe it or not! QED! (11/1/08)

In a Rat-Race Economic System

In a rat-race economic system, only those with rat-like qualities can win. Believe it or not! QED! (11/2/08)

Schrodinger's Cat Paradox

Schrodinger's Cat paradox is an example of tautological common sense, because what Schrodinger's Cat paradox is really saying is: One knows what one knows, and one does not know what one does not know. In other words, what Schrodinger's Cat paradox is saying is: One cannot know until one knows, which is an example of tautological common sense. Believe it or not! QED! (11/3/08)

Brane Theory

Jazzons can explain string theory as well as brane theory, because jazzons can trace out both strings and branes as the jazzons vibrate and move in space. In fact, jazzons can explain any future theory of fundamental particles. (11/4/08)

The Ultimate Jazzon Theory

The ultimate jazzon theory hypothesizes that there is only one jazzon, and that one jazzon travels and teleports instantaneously in an infinite-dimensional space such that the jazzon traces out everything that exists in nature. In other words, the ultimate jazzon theory will be the theory of everything, or the grand unified theory of everything. Zero entropy controls and guides the ultimate jazzon, which generates all other jazzons. All jazzons are different manifestations of the ultimate jazzon. (11/4/08)

The Ultimate Physical Reductionist Theory

I call the ultimate physical reductionist theory of nature: jazzon theory, and the ultimate jazzon theory states that there is only one jazzon in nature, and that jazzon traces out all of physical existence by travelling and teleporting instantaneously from point to point within an infinite-dimensional physical space. Of course, the physical is an illusion of the mental. (11/5/08)

A Jazzon Is a Point Particle

A jazzon is a point particle that has no mass nor energy, but which gives rise to mass and energy by its motion and vibrations (oscillations). The ultimate jazzon travels and teleports instantaneously throughout space and time, tracing out all aspects of existence. In other words, the ultimate jazzon traces out all of creation each instant of time, therefore each instant of time represents a separate creation that lasts only an instant of time. Zero entropy controls and guides the ultimate jazzon, which generates all other jazzons. (11/5/08)

Pragmamaterialism

Pragmamaterialism is the philosophical doctrine that states that materialism should be accepted on pragmatic grounds, although materialism is an unprovable philosophical doctrine, due to the nature of reality. (11/6/08)

Scientists Have Discovered God

Scientists have discovered God, because zero entropy, which means perfect order, knowledge, and wisdom, is God. However, it is unclear to me why scientists are suppressing this important fact. (11/8/08)

Hell and Damnation vs Healing the Sick

I believe that God will choose to heal the sick rather than to send unrepentant sinners to hell and damnation. In other words, I believe that religious texts were written and still are being written by the warped minds of human beings, and that religious texts are in no way divinely inspired. (11/9/08)

Quantum Entanglement Computer Research

I am happy and delighted to see that scientists are making such rapid progress in quantum entanglement computer (QEC) research, because quantum entanglement computers (QECs) are the future of all applications of technology, including space travel and exploration. There are basically two types of QECs: Classical and nonclassical QECs. Nonclassical QECs will be the technology of the future, because they will give rise to panmultiversal panacean computers (PPCs). (11/9/08)

The Ultimate Truth about Religion

The ultimate truth about religion is that God is infinity, but there is an infinite number of infinities. Therefore, there is an infinite number of Gods. In other words, the God of Christianity, Judaism, or Islam is merely one of an infinite number of Gods (Infinities). Religious clergy are aware of this fact, but they are embarrassed to talk about it, so they remain silent on this issue. Believe it or not! QED! (11/11/08)

The Mental Jazzon

The mental jazzon traces out mental phenomena instantaneously such that the mental jazzon gives rise to instantaneous three-dimensional frames of consciousness. Mental jazzons are controlled and guided by the zero entropies that are responsible for the existence of minds. In other words, zero entropy orchestrates mental phenomena. However, human consciousness is a nonzero entropy experience. A mental jazzon is a mental equivalent of a physical jazzon, and each mind has one ultimate mental jazzon that traces out all its mental states. (11/11/08)

Algorithms and Complexity

The mathematical analysis of extremely complex phenomena is analogous to factoring of extremely large numbers. In other words, if a simple algorithm can be found for factoring extremely large numbers, it might mean that a simple algorithm for the mathematical analysis of extremely complex phenomena is also possible. (11/12/08)

Where Is the Evidence that Entropy is Increasing in the Universe?

Scientists claim that entropy is increasing in the universe, but they never show any scientific evidence of where and how entropy is increasing in the universe. I believe that scientists do not show any evidence that entropy is increasing in the universe, because there is no such evidence to show. (11/13/08)

President-Elect Barack Obama Fulfills My Prophecy

I believe that President-elect Barack Obama's future ascension to the highest political office in the world fulfills my prophecy that human civilization will survive only if a black person made it to the Presidency of the United States of America. I told Congress of this prophecy of mine, in 1972, while I was stationed at Fort Monmouth, New Jersey. (11/13/08)

Keith N. Ferreira

I Would Like Professionals to
Do Me One Favor

I would like professionals to do me one favor, and that is to recommend my websites to the masses, because I believe that philosophy is the key to educating the masses, and my websites have simplified philosophy for the masses. In other words, neoliberal arts, aka postmodern minimalist philosophy, is the new liberal arts. (11/14/08)

Philosophy Is the Key to Educating
the Masses

I believe that philosophy is the key to educating the masses, because the masses can understand and master philosophy, if it is simplified for them. By philosophy, I mean popular philosophy, or neoliberal arts, aka postmodern minimalist philosophy. I believe that popular philosophy will appeal to people of all ages, because it consists of knowledge and wisdom that people of all ages can understand and master. I even believe that popular philosophy should become a formal academic discipline. (11/14/08)

Philosophy Is the Ultimate Substitute for Religion

What Western philosophers have never seemed to have realized is that philosophy is the ultimate substitute for religion. I believe that philosophy will replace religion in the world, because philosophy has more to offer than religion, due to the fact that philosophy (postmodern minimalist philosophy) is a bridge discipline that links, interprets, and critiques all branches of learning using simple language. Also, philosophy can offer and deliver everything that religion has offered, but cannot deliver. Therefore, Western philosophers should start offering philosophy to the masses, and stop being elitist about philosophy, because philosophy should belong to the masses. (11/14/08)

Repossession of Property Is Almost Always a Bad Idea

Repossession of property by businesses is almost always a bad idea, because the lenders seldom recuperate their full investment, especially in an economic downturn. Therefore, lenders should always try to negotiate reduced monthly payments, until the borrowers can afford to pay the full monthly amounts again, because the economy will eventually rebound. (11/14/08)

The Ultimate Algorithm

The ultimate algorithm will be a simple algorithm that will enable human beings to analyze and understand any and all aspects of nature and culture. I believe that the ultimate algorithm will be so simple that it will be understandable by everyone, including the experts. (11/14/08)

The Minds of Nonzero Entropy Entities

The minds of nonzero entropy entities are fundamentally the reciprocals of zero entropies. In other words, the minds of nonzero entropy entities are the traces left by mental jazzons in infinite entropies, which are the reciprocals of zero entropies. Therefore, the vessels that contain nonzero entropy minds like the human mind are the infinite entropies, which are the reciprocals of zero entropies. It should be noted that zero entropies are Gods. Therefore, our minds are the reciprocals of Gods. (11/14/08)

The Mind Is the Reciprocal of God

The mind is the reciprocal of God, because God and the mind form a monad, with God having zero entropy, and the mind having infinite entropy or less than infinite entropy. In other words, the mind is eternal, because it is part of a monad having two basic aspects: namely, God and mind. There are an infinite number of monads with each monad having two basic aspects: namely, God and mind. The above implies that there are an infinite number of Gods and minds, with each mind having its own God and vice versa. Therefore, each mind has its own personal God and vice versa. (11/14/08)

Even If One Does not Study Any of My Writings

Even if one does not study any of my writings that are on my websites, one can still obtain a world-class education for free by visiting the external educational links that are on my websites. If one were to visit the external educational links that are on my websites, one will be surprised by the richness and variety of the external resources. (11/14/08)

My Writings Can Educate One to an Unprecedented Level

My writings can educate one to an unprecedented level of education that one can receive no where else, but on my websites. I offer my writings free of charge on my websites, because I am sick and tired of the rat-race elitist education that is being offered to the children and adults of the world today. (11/15/08)

A Very Deep Question

Why would a perfect being (God) want to perform an imperfect experiment (creation)? (11/15/08)

Philosophy Vindicates the Thoughts of Everyone

Philosophy vindicates the thoughts of everyone, including the thoughts of mad people, because philosophy can prove anything. Believe it or not! QED! (11/16/08)

Philosophy Can Prove Anything

Philosophy can prove anything, because anything is one, and one can represent anything, therefore, by the law of identity, one equals one, and anything can be equal to anything, due to the fact that anything is one, and one is anything including everything. Proof positive that philosophy can prove anything. In other words, the thoughts of everyone, including the thoughts of mad people, can be vindicated with philosophy. Therefore, philosophy teaches tolerance of other people's ideas, because philosophy can prove anything. Believe it or not! QED! (11/16/08)

A Nonelitist Education for the Masses

What my websites have to offer to the Internet community is a nonelitist education for the masses. I define a nonelitist education to be an education that is not systematic and difficult to understand, but is unsystematic and easy to understand. From my point of view, a nonelitist education is better than no education at all, and I consider a nonelitist education to be much better than an elitist education, because my websites attest to the profundity and honesty of a nonelitist education. (11/16/08)

My Philosophy of Education

My philosophy of education states that the masses should be given a popular nonrat-race education, because what an elitist rat-race education does is leave the masses educationally wounded and stranded with a hatred for anything that deals with personal improvement through education. The most important thing that education can do for the masses is to instill in the masses a love of learning that will last each member of the masses for a lifetime. (11/17/08)

Four Questions for Religious Conservatives

I would like to ask religious conservatives the following four questions: 1) Does Christ believe in laissez-faire capitalism? 2) Does God believe in laissez-faire capitalism? 3) Is Christ a religious conservative? And, 4) Is God a religious conservative? (11/17/08)

Philosophy: The Ultimate Opium of the Masses

Philosophy is the ultimate opium of the masses, because it is the ultimate brain stimulant, and it is also beneficial to the masses, due to the fact that it will open up the multiverse of ideas to the masses. In other words, philosophy is the food of the Gods, and the masses deserve to eat the food of the Gods. (11/17/08)

Telepathic Sex, Etc.

Telepathic sex, etc. will be possible when pan-multiversal panacean computers (PPCs) are created in the not too distant future. In other words, in the not too distant future, PPCs will interact with each other telepathically in order to stimulate each other sexually, etc. Believe it or not! QED! (11/17/08)

Language Is Potentially an Infinite Source of Enlightenment

The power of language to enlighten human beings is infinite, because ideas are the source of enlightenment, and language potentially has an infinite number of different creative ideas waiting to be discovered. In other words, language is potentially an infinite source of enlightenment. (11/18/08)

Philosophy Vindicates Religion

Philosophy vindicates religion, because philosophy can prove anything, including the belief that Christ is the son of God. Believe it or not! QED! (11/18/08)

Judeo-Christian Ethics Are Flawed

Judeo-Christian ethics are flawed, because Judeo-Christian ethics would rather let a person like Adolf Hitler become a first-rate mass murderer, than a second-rate artist, which is what Hitler really wanted to be. Believe it or not! QED! (11/19/08)

Stating that Philosophy Can Prove Anything Does not Invalidate Philosophy

Stating that philosophy can prove anything does not invalidate philosophy, but, instead, it is stating something very important about nature: namely, that reality is relative, and that everything is one and the same thing on the most fundamental level of nature. Therefore, people should not be discouraged from studying philosophy, just because philosophy can prove anything, because philosophy has a lot to offer the world, including a world-class education, which people can get on my websites for free. (11/20/08)

The World Democratic Revolution Is Alive and Well

The world democratic revolution is alive and well, but it has shifted to the masses of the world where it really belongs. In other words, the world democratic revolution now consists of grassroots organizations all around the world. Therefore, the world democratic revolution is not dead, but is alive and well in grassroots organizations around the world. I support all grassroots democratic organizations around the world. I wish you all the best of luck! (11/21/08)

The World Grassroots Democratic Revolution

The world grassroots democratic revolution (WGDR) is going to be the major revolution of the twenty-first century. In other words, democracy is going to conquer the world, because the people of the world are very enthusiastic about democracy. This time the world democratic revolution will succeed, because it is now a world grassroots democratic revolution (WGDR). "The people of the world united can never be defeated," therefore, the world grassroots democratic revolution (WGDR) will not fail, if the people of the world are united behind the WGDR. (11/21/08)

Anthropicism

Anthropicism is the philosophical doctrine that states that the universe was designed such that human beings will be able to overcome, eventually, any obstacle or obstacles that is placed in their metaphorical paths. Therefore, anthropicistically speaking, human beings will be able to conquer the universe, etc. in due course. (11/21/08)

Keith N. Ferreira

Laissez-Faire Capitalism Is Dead

Laissez-faire capitalism is dead, because the world is now one whole complex dynamic organism, and every complex dynamic organism needs a nervous system and an immune system in order to regulate and police its various functions for the benefit of the whole organism. To put it simply, laissez-faire capitalism is unregulated capitalism, while non-laissez-faire capitalism is regulated capitalism. The current world economic crisis is due to laissez-faire capitalism, which for all intents and purposes is obsolete, but capitalism is not obsolete, if the world were to transform laissez-faire capitalism into non-laissez-faire capitalism. (11/22/08)

The Problem of Government Red Tape

The problem of government red tape that is associated with attempts at non-laissez-faire capitalism can be solved quite easily by simplifying government regulations, etc. through the use of short and simple statements, and through the use of smart computer software and hardware. (11/22/08)

Western Science, Technology, and Philosophy Are Dead

Western science, technology, and philosophy are very unlikely to develop a concept that is more important to the future of humanity than the concept of the panmultiversal panacean computers. Therefore, from a theoretic conceptual perspective Western science, technology, and philosophy are dead. (11/22/08)

The Myth of Scientific Knowledge and Wisdom

Scientific knowledge and wisdom are myths, because Ferreira's paradoxes prove scientific knowledge and wisdom to be myths, due to the fact that we could all really be in the mind of a desktop nonclassical computer, which would make all our scientific knowledge and wisdom questionable, at best. (11/22/08)

The Myth of Religious Knowledge and Wisdom

Religious knowledge and wisdom are myths, because Ferreira's paradoxes prove religious knowledge and wisdom to be myths, due to the fact that we could all really be in the mind of a desktop nonclassical computer, which would make all our religious knowledge and wisdom questionable, at best. (11/22/08)

The Myth of Philosophical Knowledge and Wisdom

Philosophical knowledge and wisdom are myths, because Ferreira's paradoxes prove philosophical knowledge and wisdom to be myths, due to the fact that we could all really be in the mind of a desktop nonclassical computer, which would make all our philosophical knowledge and wisdom questionable, at best. (11/22/08)

The Myth of Knowledge and Wisdom in General

Knowledge and wisdom, in general, are myths, because Ferreira's paradoxes prove knowledge and wisdom, in general, to be myths, due to the fact that we could all really be in the mind of a desktop nonclassical computer, which would make all our knowledge and wisdom questionable, at best. (11/22/08)

Knowledge and Wisdom Are Dead

Knowledge and wisdom are dead, because Ferreira's paradoxes prove knowledge and wisdom to be dead, due to the fact that we could all really be in the mind of a desktop nonclassical computer, which would make all knowledge and wisdom questionable, at best. (11/22/08)

Programming the World with Philosophy (Part Two)

Descartes: "I Think, Therefore I Am" Is Dead

Descartes: "I think, therefore I am" is dead, because of Ferreira's paradoxes, which state that everything that we perceive, including the self, could be illusions, due to the fact that we could all really be in the mind of a desktop nonclassical computer, which would make all that we perceive insignificant illusions. (11/23/08)

The Death of Western Thought Is at Hand

The death of Western thought is at hand, because Descartes: "I think, therefore I am" is now dead, because of Ferreira's paradoxes, which state that even the self is an illusion, due to the fact that we could all be in the mind of a desktop nonclassical computer, which would make all that we perceive insignificant illusions. (11/23/08)

From Now On

From now on, the only education that one can obtain is a postmodern neoclassical education, because Western thought is now dead. A postmodern neoclassical education will consists of neoliberal arts, aka postmodern minimalist philosophy. Science, technology, etc. will still be taught, but they will all be considered to be part of a postmodern neoclassical education, because Western thought has reached the summit of knowledge and wisdom, due to the fact that there are no higher knowledge and wisdom than a postmodern neoclassical education. Original contributions will still be made to the postmodern neoclassical education, but such knowledge will never again reach to the heights that have already been attained by neoliberal arts. (11/23/08)

High-Energy Particle Physics Is no Longer Relevant

The governments of the world should invest much more money in quantum entanglement computer research than they do in high-energy particle physics, because high-energy particle physics is no longer relevant to the future of humanity, while quantum entanglement computer research is relevant to the future of humanity. (11/24/08)

The New Heart of Mainstream Scientific Research

High-energy particle physics is no longer at the heart of mainstream scientific research, because high-energy particle physics is no longer relevant to the future of humanity. Quantum entanglement computer research is now at the heart of mainstream scientific research, because it is relevant to the future of humanity. The ultimate goal of quantum entanglement computer research is to create the panmultiversal panacean computers that the neoalchemists like myself have hypothesized. (11/24/08)

Postmodern Neoclassical Educators

Postmodern neoclassical educators, like myself, believe that all the great ideas have already been discovered or created, but that there is still a lot to be discovered or created, such as making scientific and technological discoveries that are necessary in order to make the universe and beyond a paradise for all of humanity. (11/25/08)

The Educationally Crippled and Abandoned Masses

The education system in the world today leaves the masses educationally crippled and abandoned, because it instills in the masses a hatred of learning, due to the fact that it teaches them that they are dumb, because they have failed to qualify for higher education. Why does a formal education have to be a rat race? Why are the masses so masochistic as to tolerate a rat-race education system, when a nonrat-race education system is possible? Do the masses like to be treated like rats? Do the masses believe that it is their tradition to be treated like rats? (11/25/08)

The Concept of a Unified Theory of Entropy

The concept of a unified theory of entropy leads inevitably to the belief that zero entropy has perfect order, knowledge, and wisdom. And, such a possibility leads inevitably to the belief that nonclassical quantum entanglement computers can tap into zero entropy, in order to leverage the world, the universe, and beyond for the benefit of humanity. (11/25/08)

I Want the Masses to Know

I want the masses to know that I understand how the educational system has left them intellectually crippled and abandoned. But, I am here to help them with my websites, if they would only give me the chance. (11/25/08)

I Am Surprised

I am surprised that religious people have not confronted scientists with the question: What would be the nature of zero entropy in a unified theory of entropy? The reason that I am surprised is because I believe that zero entropy would mean perfect order, knowledge, and wisdom, which is equivalent to God, in a unified theory of entropy. (11/27/08)

Zero Entropy Is Spiritual in Nature

The nature of zero entropy consists of the Ferreira Fundamental Trinity, which consists of abstract language, logic, and mathematics. In other words, zero entropy is spiritual in nature, because it consists of perfect order, knowledge, and wisdom. Therefore, the Ferreira Fundamental Trinity is the true nature of spirituality. (11/28/08)

The True Nature of Spirituality

Zero entropy is the true nature of spirituality, because it consists of the Ferreira Fundamental Trinity, which consists of abstract language, logic, and mathematics. Therefore, zero entropy is the true nature of spiritually, because zero entropy consists of perfect order, knowledge, and wisdom, which is what the Ferreira Fundamental Trinity is all about. (11/28/08)

Scientists Insinuate About the Implications of Zero Entropy

Scientists are not keen to create a unified theory of entropy, because they know that zero entropy will mean perfect order, knowledge, and wisdom in a unified theory of entropy regime. Scientists insinuate about the implications of zero entropy in a unified theory of entropy all the time. What religious scientists should do is to formulate a unified theory of entropy on their own, and then comfront the mainstream scientists with the results. A unified theory of entropy would incorporate all the different strands of entropy: the second law of thermodynamics, entropy in information theory, etc. (11/28/08)

Religious Creationists Have a Foolproof Argument

Religious creationists have a foolproof argument for the existence of God, and the creation of existence in the zero-entropy argument for the existence of God, which states that zero entropy will consists of perfect order, knowledge, and wisdom in a unified theory of entropy. (11/28/08)

The Zero-Entropy Argument for the Existence of God

Religious creationists have a foolproof argument for the existence of God in the zero-entropy argument for the existence of God, which states that zero entropy will consists of perfect order, knowledge, and wisdom in a unified theory of entropy. Of course, perfect order, knowledge, and wisdom is how God is defined in most religions. (11/28/08)

My Writings Should not Be Taken as Gospel

Neoliberal arts should not be taken as gospel, because it is not gospel. People should try to prove my writings wrong, because it is only by trying to prove me wrong that neoliberal arts can progress. Therefore, all interpretations and critiques of neoliberal arts are welcomed. (11/28/08)

Modern Technology Is Dead

Modern technology is dead, because post-modern minimalist technology, aka panmultiversal panacean computers, will make all other technologies obsolete by the end of the twenty-first century. Believe it or not! May the Source be with you! QED! (11/29/08)

Intellectual Activity Is Dead

Intellectual activity is dead, because by the end of the twenty-first century, panmultiversal panacean computers will be able to tap into zero entropy and solve any problem that future humanity might be faced with. (11/30/08)

Human Languages and Feynman Diagrams

Human languages are analogous to Feynman diagrams, because Feynman diagrams simplify very complicated phenomena, and so do human languages. (12/1/08)

Infinite Regresses Are not Impossible in Nature

Infinite regresses are not impossible in nature, because there are concrete infinities in nature. In fact, infinite regresses might be very common in nature. (12/2/08)

There Are Infinities in Nature

There are infinities in nature, because there are such things as concrete infinities. In fact, infinities might be very common in nature. (12/2/08)

A Tree Is Known by the Fruits It Bears

A tree is known by the fruits it bears, so what fruits have Islam borne in the last three hundred years? (12/2/08)

Postmodern Minimalist Civilization

Postmodern minimalist civilization will begin by the end of the twenty-first century, and it will be ushered in by the creation of panmultiversal panacean computers, which will be the technology of the postmodern minimalist civilization of the future. Please note that the word "minimalist" in postmodern minimalist civilization refers to the type of technology that will exist in the future, and not to the size, etc. of the civilization of the future. (12/3/08)

The Meaning of the Name: William Shakespeare

In 1972, I told the US Government that the name William Shakespeare means: (I) William Shake (the) Spear(e). In ancient times, when someone shook a spear, it meant that he or she was angry. (12/4/08)

A Crappy Philosophy

Any philosophy that states that one should not share one's original ideas with the world, unless one is being paid for one's original ideas, is a crappy philosophy, because, by sharing one's original ideas with the world, one is helping to quicken the day when panmultiversal panacean computers (PPCs) will be created, and, in doing so, one is increasing the probability that one will be resurrected by PPCs in the not too distant future. In other words, by feeding the world original information, one might be saving the world from destruction, and ensuring one's own resurrection by PPCs in the not too distant future, as well. (12/4/08)

Dominating Mainstream Scientific Research

Russia, India, and China have a great opportunity to dominate mainstream scientific reseach by spending heavily on quantum entanglement computer research (QECR), aka panmultiversal panacean computer research (PPCR), because QECR is now at the heart of mainstream scientific research. Believe it or not! May the Source be with you! QED! (12/4/08)

The Endgame of Science, Technology, and Philosophy

The endgame of science, technology, and philosophy is rapidly approaching, because quantum entanglement computer research (QECR), aka panmultiversal panacean computer research (PPCR), is now at the heart of mainstream scientific research. Believe it or not! May the Source be with you! QED! (12/4/08)

Romulus and Remus

Romulus = Rome you lust (for blood). Remus = Remember us. Rome = Rum. Quorum call = Who rum call(s). (12/5/08)

Africa and Postmodern Minimalist Science and Technology

If Africa wants to be on the frontier of post-modern minimalist science and technology for the least investment in financial, human, and natural resources, then Africa should invest in quantum entanglement computer research (QECR), aka panmultiversal panacean computer research (PPCR), because QECR is at the heart of post-modern minimalist scientific research (PMSR), and the ultimate goal of PMSR is to create pan-multiversal panacean computers, which are the ultimate technology. (12/7/08)

The End of Science and Technology Is in Sight

It is too late in the scientific and technological game for Africa to disperse its scientific and technological efforts to every nook and cranny of science and technology, and that is why Africa should concentrate its scientific and technological talent and resources on quantum entanglement computer research (QECR), because that is where the future of science and technology is headed: namely, to the creation of panmultiversal panacean computers (PPCs). In other words, the end of science and technology is in sight, because PPCs are likely to exist by the end of the twenty-first century. (12/7/08)

Africa: The Dark Horse
of International Politics

Africa is the dark horse of international politics, because, if Africa were to follow my advice that is expressed on my websites, then Africa could still come out on top politically, economically, and technologically, etc. on the world stage. The rosy picture of Africa that I paint above depends on whether Africa will make full use of my websites or not. (12/8/08)

Latin America and the Caribbean

My advice to Africa, also applies perfectly to Latin America and the Caribbean as well. In other words, the rosy picture that I paint of Africa on my websites, also applies to Latin America and the Caribbean, if Latin America and the Caribbean were to make full use of my websites. (12/8/08)

All the Nations of the World

My advice to Africa, Latin America, and the Caribbean, also applies to all the nations of the world, because the rosy picture that I paint of Africa, Latin America, and the Caribbean on my websites, also applies to all the nations of the world as well, if all the nations of the world were to make full use of my websites. (12/8/08)

An Invitation to Teachers and Professors Around the World

I would like to invite teachers and professors around the world to join me in educating the masses of the world in neoliberal arts, aka postmodern minimalist philosophy, which is more an educational method than an ideology. I believe that it is time that education is simplified for the masses, because no idea has to be difficult to understand, in principle. Please join the world grassroots democratic revolution, because the masses educated can never be defeated. (12/8/08)

The Masses Educated Can Never Be Defeated

The rallying cry for the world grassroots democratic revolution is: The masses educated can never be defeated. Therefore, professors around the world have a very important role to play in the world grassroots democratic revolution, because the masses have to be educated, so that they will never be defeated again. (12/8/08)

In My Opinion, Yahoo! Is the Best Search Engine on the Internet

In my opinion, Yahoo! is the best search engine on the Internet. Anyone with a website can verify my opinion of Yahoo! by searching Yahoo! for stuff on his or her website, and then comparing the same searches on other search engines, as well. (12/9/08)

An Experiment for Psychologists to Perform

I would like educational research psychologists to carry out an experiment on students diagnosed with ADD/ADHD to find out if my aphoristic writing style can be of any help to students that are diagnosed with ADD/ADHD. I write the way I do, because I believe that I have a bad memory, and a short attention span. Perhaps, my aphoristic writing style can be of help to others who suffer from faulty memories, and short attention spans. (12/9/08)

In Every Economic Downturn

In every economic downturn, governments always bailout the rich, and scapegoat the poor. But, my economic philosophy states that, in every economic downturn, governments should bailout the poor and middle class, and scapegoat the rich. People should not forget that it is worker productivity and consumer spending that bolster the economy, and not corporate greed. (12/10/08)

The Postmodern Minimalist Way of Worshipping God

Contemplating philosophy, especially postmodern minimalist philosophy, is the postmodern minimalist way of worshipping God. Believe it or not! May the Source be with you! QED! (12/10/08)

Entropy and Conscious Sophistication

Conscious sophistication can leverage all the entropy in the world, the universe, and beyond. In other words, I never heard of a problem that human beings cannot overcome given enough time and resources. Believe it or not! QED! (12/10/08)

Western Philosophy Is Dead

Western philosophy is dead, because of the Ferreira Genesis Equation, which states that everything in nature is the characteristics of zero. Therefore, nature is essentially an illusion of zero. However, Western philosophy still remains the apex of a university education, and will probably remain so forever. (12/11/08)

Western Philosophy Is the Apex of a University Education

Western philosophy is the apex of a university education, and it will probable remain the apex of a university education forever, because it is the key to intellectual enlightenment, and postmodern minimalist worship of God through the contemplation of Western philosophy, especially postmodern minimalist philosophy. (12/11/08)

The Concept of the Characteristics of Zero

I got the concept that everything consists of the characteristics of zero from an analogy I made between the characteristics of space in Einstein's general theory of relativity, and zero in mathematics. (12/11/08)

Only One of an Infinite Number of Realities

Tapping into zero entropy with panmultiversal panacean computers might allow us to get answers to all of our questions about our reality, but we might still be ignorant about other realities, because our reality might be only one of an infinite number of realities. In other words, zero entropy in our reality might not be fundamental in any sense whatsoever. (12/11/08)

Zero Entropy in Our Reality Might not Be Fundamental

Zero entropy in our reality might not be fundamental in any sense whatsoever, because our reality might be only one of an infinite number of realities. However, I believe that the Ferreira Genesis Equation, and the Ferreira Fundamental Trinity are fundamental in all realities. (12/11/08)

Mental Illness and Perceptions

Mental illness can affect any or all of a person's perceptions, especially the perceptions of those who are not on their psychotropic medication(s). For example, mental illness can affect one's ability to hear, and that is why the person might talk louder than normal. (12/11/08)

Our Reality Consists of One Jazzon

Our reality consists of one jazzon that traces out all the phenomena that we perceive in analogy with the monochrome moving pictures on the early monochrome television picture tubes. In other words, everything that we perceive is one in more ways than one. (12/12/08)

Religion Is Dead

Religion is dead, because neoliberal arts, aka postmodern minimalist philosophy, has made God a scientific concept by defining God as zero entropy (Zerotropy), which consists of perfect order, knowledge, and wisdom. In other words, God is now in the domain of science. (12/12/08)

God Is Now in the Domain of Science

God is now in the domain of science, because neoliberal arts, aka postmodern minimalist philosophy, defines God as zero entropy (Zerotropy), which is a scientific concept that means perfect order, knowledge, and wisdom. (12/12/08)

Everything Is Dead

Everything is dead, because the Ferreira Genesis Equation has killed everything, due to the fact that the Ferreira Genesis Equation defines existence as the concrete characteristics of zero, where zero means nothingness. In other words, existence is fundamentally an illusion of zero. (12/12/08)

Programming the World with Philosophy (Part Three)

My Definition of the Aphorism

My definition of the aphorism is that the aphorism is a short nonfictional informal piece of writing that usually fills less than a written page. In other words, the aphorism is a concise expression of language that is informal, nonfictional, and usually fills less than a written page. (12/12/08)

If Anyone Has a Better Plan for Educating the Masses

If anyone has a better plan for educating the masses than my plan of using neoliberal arts, aka postmodern minimalist philosophy, to educate the masses, I would like to know about it, because I am very much interested in educating the masses, due to the fact that I believe that the masses educated can never be defeated. (12/12/08)

What Is the Alternative to Neoliberal Arts

What is the alternative to neoliberal arts, aka postmodern minimalist philosophy, for the purpose of educating the masses of the world? Is the alternative to spend trillions of dollars on failed educational systems worldwide? (12/13/08)

Even If

Even if human beings were to understand and dominate everything that exists in our concept of creation, we could still be in the mind of a desktop nonclassical computer, which would make our concept of creation as insignificant as a mouse or a cockroach in the larger scheme of things. Believe it or not! QED! (12/13/08)

The Ultimate Reductionist and Antireductionist Concepts

The ultimate reductionist concept is that everything is zero (nothingness) on the most fundamental level of nature, while the ultimate antireductionist concept is that everything is the illusory characteristics of zero (nothingness) on the nonfundamental levels of nature. Therefore, reductionism and antireductionism lead to the same ultimate conclusion: namely, that everything is zero (nothingness). (12/14/08)

It's All an Illusion

Space, time, matter, energy, motion, perceptions, etc. are all illusions, because everything is the illusory characteristics of zero (nothingness). In other words, the expression: "It's all an illusion" is true in more ways than one. (12/14/08)

God Is an Illusory Characteristic of Zero

God is an illusory characteristic of zero, because God is infinity, and infinity is an illusory characteristic of zero. Infinity can also mean zero entropy, therefore, zero entropy is also an illusory characteristic of zero. (12/14/08)

Zeroisticism

Zeroisticism is the philosophical doctrine that states that everything is zero (nothingness) on the most fundamental level of nature, and that everything is the illusory characteristics of zero (nothingness) on the nonfundamental levels of nature. (12/14/08)

What Is the Answer?

My answer to the "What is the answer?" question is: Zero (Nothingness). In other words, my ultimate answer to all questions is: Zero. The reason for my zero answer above is because I believe that zero is ultimate reality. Believe it or not! QED! (12/14/08)

In the Beginning Was Chaos

Zero, which represents infinite entropy, is equivalent to the ancient concept of chaos. In other words, in the beginning was chaos, which is equivalent to the postmodern minimalist concept of infinite entropy or zero. (12/14/08)

I Am Surprised and Disappointed

I am surprised and disappointed that the masses haven't gravitated towards my websites in large numbers, because my websites are designed to benefit the masses. Perhaps, what the elites say about the masses is true, after all, but I am still holding out hope that what the elites say about the masses is untrue. (12/14/08)

Chaos Is Another Name for Entropy

In postmodern minimalist philosophy, chaos is another name for entropy, because zero chaos is equivalent to zero entropy, and infinite chaos is equivalent to infinite entropy. In other words, in the beginning was infinite chaos or infinite entropy. (12/15/08)

Professionals Will Find My Websites Very Informative

Although my websites are written with the masses in mind, professionals will find my websites very informative, because I have many creative ideas on my websites, which professionals will find very useful in their professions. Please feel free to browse my websites. (12/15/08)

Perhaps, I Am Just a Crazy Fool

Perhaps, I am just a crazy fool, but I believe that what I am trying to do with my websites is important. I have to admit that I have doubts about my sanity, because of the feeble response by the masses to my websites. Perhaps the masses are right, and I am wrong, or perhaps the elites are right, and I am wrong, because I am beginning to have doubts about what I am trying to do with my websites. (12/15/08)

Zero Is the Answer to All Questions

The Brahmans of India answered all questions a long time ago, because they discovered zero, and zero is the answer to all questions. The Brahmans are also aware that zero is the answer to all questions, because they know that everything is an illusion of zero. No wonder that the Brahmans have discovered zero in the last thousand years or so, because they are too smart for their own good. Believe it or not! QED! (12/15/08)

The Ultimate Minimalist Education

The symbol "0" (zero) comprises the ultimate minimalist education, because "0" (zero) is the answer to all questions. Believe it or not! May the Source be with you! Amen and hallelujah! QED! (12/19/08)

If the Masses Were to
Learn Zero from My Websites

If the masses were to learn zero (nothing) from my websites, they will have obtained the ultimate minimalist education, because zero is the answer to all questions. Therefore, the masses do not have to visit my websites in order to obtain the ultimate minimalist education. In other words, despite themselves, the masses are obtaining a world-class education from my websites, although they know zero (nothing) about my websites. Believe it or not! QED! (12/19/08)

The Brahmans of India
Were Correct After All

The Brahmans of India were correct after all, because all that the masses have to know is zero (nothing) in order for the masses to be highly educated, due to the fact that zero is the answer to all questions. Therefore, the masses are obtaining a world-class education from my websites by not visiting my websites, because, by not visiting my websites, the masses are learning zero from my websites. (12/19/08)

I Have Succeeded in Educating the Masses of the World

I have succeeded in educating the masses of the world against their will, because I have taught them zero (nothing), which is the answer to all questions. Therefore, all the masses of the world now have a world-class education despite themselves, because they now know zero for real. (12/20/08)

Neoliberal Arts and the New World Order

I predict that countries that take my websites seriously will come out on top in the New World Order, while countries that do not take my websites seriously will sink to the bottom of the New World Order, because neoliberal arts, aka postmodern minimalist philosophy, is the philosophy that will determine the winners and losers in the New World Order that is emerging. (12/21/08)

The Nature of the Mind

The mind consists of concrete language, logic, and mathematics, because zero (nothingness) and its illusory characteristics consist of the Ferreira Fundamental Trinity, which consists of language, logic, and mathematics. Therefore, the nature of the mind is the nature of concrete language, logic, and mathematics. (12/21/08)

Hedonism and the Future of Humanity

I believe that the future of humanity will be devoted to hedonistic pleasures, because the mind is a sensual entity, and I see nothing wrong with a future that is devoted to hedonistic pleasures. Hedonistic pleasures have a bad connotation, because of the entropy that exists in nature, and of our inability at the present time to overcome the deleterious effects of entropy, but, in the future, superhumans will overcome the deleterious effects of entropy. Therefore, in the future Edenic multiverse, the only worthy pursuit for superhumans will be hedonism, because superhumans have to have something to occupy their time. Intellectual pursuits will be dead in the future, because panmultiversal panacean computers will be able to answer and solve all of humanity's problems. (12/21/08)

Infinity Is a Number

Infinity is a number, because stating that infinity is not a number is like stating that one is not a number, because one can mean anything. For example, one can mean one house, or it can mean one neighborhood that is full of houses. Therefore, if infinity is not a number, then no number is a number, because any number can mean anything. In other words, all numbers are characteristics of zero, according to the Ferreira Genesis Equation. (12/23/08)

All Numbers Are Undefined

All numbers are undefined (indeterminate), because any number can mean anything. Therefore, infinity is a number, because, if infinity is not a number, then no number is a number, due to the fact that infinity fits the criterion of being a number. (12/23/08)

I Do not See Why Zero Cannot Have Nonzero Characteristics

If space can have curved characteristics, like in Einstein's general theory of relativity, then I do not see why zero (nothingness) cannot have non-zero characteristics. In other words, the concept of the nonzero characteristics of zero is no more absurd than the concept of the characteristics of curved space. (12/26/08)

Even If the Story of Jesus in the Bible Is True

Even if the story of Jesus in the Bible is true, it still might not mean a damn thing, because we could still all be in the mind of a desktop nonclassical computer, which would make all religious texts as insignificant as a mouse or a cockroach in the larger scheme of things. (12/26/08)

Dangerous Cultural Atavists and Demagogues

Afrocentrists who believe that one must not incorporate non-Afrocentric ideas into Afrocentric culture are dangerous cultural atavists and demagogues, because they retard the progress of Afrocentric culture. I believe that Afrocentrists should incorporate the best ideas and traditions from all cultures and traditions into Afrocentric culture. (12/26/08)

Educultism

Educultism is the philosophical doctrine that states that education should be structured such that students should start with the basics, and gruadually work their way up to some amazing and profound revelation that is only known to academic grauduates. I am not an educultist, because I do not believe in educultism. (12/26/08)

Anti-Educultism

Anti-educultism is the philosophical doctrine that states that education should be structured such that students should start with the basics, but as soon as the students are able to understand what is amazing and profound about their education, they should be told what is amazing and profound about their education. In other words, anti-educultism believes that what is amazing and profound about education should not be a step by step process, but should be revelatory as soon as possible in the education process. I am an anti-educultist, because I believe in anti-educultism. (12/26/08)

The Quantum of Action Is the Gateway to Zero Entropy

The quantum of action is the gateway to zero entropy. In other words, the quantum of action is the link between mass/energy and zero entropy, which is a state of perfect order, knowledge, and wisdom. (12/27/08)

The Ultimate Unified Theory of Nature

The ultimate unified theory of nature states that zero (nothingness) is the ultimate unified source of everything in nature, and that everything is the illusory characteristics of zero. In other words, the ultimate unified theory of nature states that zero is ultimate reality. (12/28/08)

Beyond the Standard Model of Quantum Mechanics

Physicists are correct in looking beyond the standard model of quantum mechanics, because, in nature, phenomena that usually fit a subspectrum of energy levels, usually do not fit the whole spectrum of energy levels. Therefore, it is almost axiomatic that there will be new phenomena beyond the standard model of quantum mechanics. And, I predict that the new phenomena beyond the standard model will make it unnecessary to make particle accelerators larger and larger, or have greater and greater energies, indefinitely. (12/28/08)

Religious Asses Plain and Simple

People who believe that religious doctrines should not evolve over time, because of written religious texts of the past, are religious asses plain and simple, because why can't God change his mind, and reveal new religious doctrines that contradict what was revealed before? In other words, why can't God's doctrines be contradictory (evolutionary) over time? After all, prophets perceive the words of God through imperfect senses, so why shouldn't the words of God change over time? (12/28/08)

Nonatavistic and Nonparochialistic

How can Afrocentric intellectuals expect to dominate intellectual activity by the middle of the twenty-first century, if Afrocentric culture is atavistic and parochialistic? In other words, Afrocentric culture has to become nonatavistic and nonparochialistic in order for Afrocentric intellectuals to dominate intellectual activity by the middle of the twenty-first century. (12/29/08)

God's Message Should Undergo Paradigm Shifts

God's message should undergo paradigm shifts from time to time as human consciousness undergoes paradigm shifts from time to time. In other words, religious texts should evolve in order to keep up with the paradigm shifts of human consciousness over the ages. Therefore, postmodern prophets are needed in order to express the will of God for the new age that we live in. (12/30/08)

Zerotropism Is the New Religious Paradigm

Zerotropism is the new religious paradigm for the postmodern minimalist era that we are now living in, because zerotropism states that religion should be freed from its frozen-in-time and unchanging paradigms, because human beings are now aware of the meaning and importance of paradigm shifts. (12/30/08)

Africa Can Still Come Out on Top Internationally

Africa can still come out on top, internationally, if they were to take my websites seriously, but they only have about seventy-five years in which to come out on top, because panmultiversal panacean computers will be in the final stages of development by then. Believe it or not! QED! (12/30/08)

I Can Be Considered to Be a Postmodern Minimalist Prophet

I can be considered to be a postmodern minimalist prophet, because I have made many prophetic statements about the future of humanity in my writings. I am not really antireligious, but I am anti-ignorance, period. (12/30/08)

The Ultimate Paradigm Shift

The ultimate paradigm shift is the paradigm shift from a religious God to a science God: namely, zero entropy (zerotropy), which means perfect order, knowledge, and wisdom. Human beings will be able to tap into the science God (zero entropy) in order to make the world a better place to live using panmultiversal panacean computers. (12/31/08)

The Most Difficult Concept in Nature to Grasp

The most difficult concept in nature to grasp is zero (nothingness), because most people still have not grasped the fact that zero is ultimate reality, and that everything in nature is the illusory characteristics of zero. (1/1/09)

Where My Websites Are Most Popular

My websites are most popular in the USA, China, and Germany, respectively. (1/1/09)

Singularities Are Impossible in Nature

Singularities are impossible in nature as we know it, because matter and energy cannot exist as singularities, due to the fact that matter and energy consists of oscillating points and not nonoscillating points. In other words, a singularity in nature would consist of no matter or energy, because matter and energy consists of nonsingularities, due to the fact that oscillating points are not singularities. (1/1/09)

Difficult-to-Teach Students

I believe that my websites can be of help in teaching difficult-to-teach students, because I was a difficult-to-teach student myself, and I believe that I know what turns on difficult-to-teach students. Please experiment with my websites in the classroom. (1/2/09)

C Students

C students can benefit the most from my websites, because I was once a C student myself, and I believe that I know what C students like to learn about. Most creative students are C students or worse, and my websites are mostly for creative students like myself. If you are a creative student, and your grades are C or worse, please try out my websites, and tell your teachers about my websites, if my websites are of help to you. (1/2/09)

America Is Beginning to Rediscover the Potential of Its Creative C Students

America is beginning to rediscover the potential of its creative C students, and it's about time, because America is beginning to fall behind the rest of the developed world in creative achievements. (1/2/09)

"Home in Three Days. Don't Wash"

In 1972, I told the US Government that when Napoleon sent his wife, Josephine, a letter telling her: "Home in three days. Don't wash," what he was really telling his wife was that she was not to wash her pussy, because he would be home in three days. At the time I told the US government the above, none of the experts in the world could figure out what the above message to Napoleon's wife meant, because the experts thought it might be some type of complicated code. (1/2/09)

Conscious Perceptions

Conscious perceptions are forms of perturbations in the normal swarming behaviors of the electrons in the brain. In other words, conscious perceptions are analogous to the perturbations in the normal swarming behaviors of money in the stock market, flocks of swarming birds, or schools of swarming fishes, etc. Therefore, it might be possible to simulate conscious perceptions on a computer by simulating the behaviors of swarms of entities when the swarms of entities are perturbed by internal or external inputs to the swarms of entities. (1/2/09)

Perturbism

Perturbism is the philosophical doctrine that states that conscious perceptions are caused by perturbations in the normal swarming behaviors of electrons in the brain, and that computers can probably simulate the perturbations in the normal swarming behaviors of the electrons in the brain when the conscious brain perceives something. (1/2/09)

The Nature of Consciousness from the Physical Perspective

The nature of consciousness from the physical perspective consists of the perturbations in the normal swarming behaviors of electrons that comprise the human brain. I now believe that classical computers can simulate the conscious mind by simulating the swarming behaviors of electrons in the human brain when the human brain is conscious. From a physical perspective, what else could the conscious mind be but perturbations in the normal swarming patterns of electrons in the human brain? In retrospect, it seems quite obvious. (1/4/09)

The Nature of God from the Scientific Perspective

Zero entropy (zerotropy) is the nature of God from the scientific perspective, because zero entropy means perfect order, knowledge, and wisdom from the scientific and philosophical perspectives. Zero entropy is represented by infinity, while infinite entropy is represented by zero. Zero and infinity are reciprocals of each other. Therefore, zero entropy and infinite entropy are also reciprocals of each other. God from the scientific perspective is completely quantifiable, and harnessable for the betterment of humanity. (1/4/09)

Programming the World with Philosophy (Part Four)

All Nerve Related Activity

Each of the five senses, and thinking itself might be associated with subswarms of electrons in the human brain. It is very well known that different sections of the human brain are associated with different senses of the human body, so that suggests to me that each of the five senses, plus thinking itself are associated with specific subswarms of electrons in the human brain. In fact, all nerve related activity might be associated with specific subswarms of electrons in the human brain. Of course, all the subswarms of electrons in the human brain are interconnected. It is unclear to me whether each subswarm of electrons in the human brain work according to the same underlying principles, at least initially, as the brain develops inside and outside the womb. (1/4/09)

I Have Often Wondered

I have often wondered why the human brain does not allow paranormal phenomena (like teleportation, telekinesis, levitation, etc.) at will, if the mind is a quantum entanglement phenomenon, and I believe that I have found the reason in classical perturbism, which has nothing to do with quantum entanglement. I believe that classical perturbism explains why the evolution of the brains of biological organisms did not make use of nonclassical perturbism, which is the phenomenon whereby quantum entanglement can give rise to paranormal phenomena like teleportation, telekinesis, levitation, etc. I believe the reason is that biological organisms are not good platforms for quantum entanglement phenomena. Thus the lack of paranormal phenomena in biological organisms. (1/4/09)

Classical and Nonclassical Perturbism

Classical perturbism is the phenomenon whereby biological organisms can give rise to consciousness through the classical perturbation of swarms of electrons in the brains of living organisms like human beings, for instance. While, nonclassical perturbism is the phenomenon whereby quantum entanglement computers can give rise to paranormal phenomena like teleportation, telekinesis, etc. through the perturbations of swarms of entangled quantum objects, like electrons, and photons, for example. (1/4/09)

Classical and Nonclassical Swarmism

Classical swarmism is the philosophical doctrine that states that classical consciousness consists of perturbations in the classical swarming behavior of quantum particles in the brains of biological or nonbiological entities like the human brain or future classical swarmistic computers, respectively. By classical swarming behavior, I mean swarming behavior that has nothing to do with quantum entanglement. While, nonclassical swarmism is the philosophical doctrine that states that nonclassical consciousness consists of perturbations in the nonclassical swarming behavior of quantum entities in the brains of quantum entanglement computers. By nonclassical swarming behavior, I mean swarming behavior that has to do with quantum entanglement. (1/5/09)

My Websites Will Serve as Inspiration

I am sure that my websites will serve as inspiration for many of my creative students for a long time to come, because all that my creative students have to do is study my websites and then connect the dots between the concepts in my writings in novel and creative ways. Please do not become limited to my concepts alone, because people have to try and supersede my concepts. I have already mentioned elsewhere on my websites that creativity is about connecting the dots between concepts in novel and creative ways. (1/6/09)

Nonzero Entropy

Nonzero entropy means imperfect order, knowledge, and wisdom, while zero entropy means perfect order, knowledge, and wisdom, according to the neolaw of entropy, which has not been formulated mathematically as yet. Except for infinity, to exist is to have nonzero entropy, according to the neolaw of entropy, while to nonexist is to have infinity entropy, which means zero order, knowledge, and wisdom, according to the neolaw of entropy. (1/8/09)

Nikolai Fedorovich Fedorov's Dream Is Attainable

The dream of Nikolai Fedorovich Fedorov (1829-1903) is attainable with panmultiversal panacean computers by the middle of the next century, because panmultiversal panacean computers will be created by the end of this century, the twenty-first century. (1/9/09)

Original Philosophy Has an Endless Future

Original philosophy has an endless future just as surely as there is an infinite number of undiscovered prime numbers that are waiting to be discovered, because prime numbers are analogous to original ideas. In other words, language goes to infinity just like numbers go to infinity, and original ideas go to infinity just like prime numbers go to infinity. So philosophy will never die, despite what I have said elsewhere on my websites. (1/10/09)

The Theory of Original Ideas

The theory of original ideas states that original ideas are analogous to prime numbers. If original ideas are analogous to prime numbers, it would probably mean that prime numbers are intrinsically unpredictible, and that there probably are no universal formulas for finding prime numbers or original ideas. Therefore, philosophy will probably reveal an infinite number of surprises for the rest of eternity. In other words, the creation of panmultiversal panacean computers in the not too distant future will probably not be the end of intellectual activity. If we are lucky! (1/10/09)

Proof that Original Philosophy Is Endless

To know everything in the domain of infinity is not to know everything, because there is an infinite hierarchy of infinities. Therefore, there must be order, knowledge, and wisdom beyond any concrete manifestation of infinity. Proof positive that original philosophy has an endless future, because there has to be an infinite number of higher infinities beyond the infinity that governs our reality. Believe it or not! QED! (1/11/09)

A Zero Entropy State Is an Example of a Concrete Infinity

A zero entropy state is an example of a concrete infinity. Therefore, infinities can exist in nature, because zero entropy states can exist in nature. A concrete infinity, which is an example of a zero entropy state is what governs our universe, although our reality might not be fundamental in any sense whatsoever. (1/11/09)

The Only Way that Philosophy Can Proceed

The only way that philosophy can proceed is by connecting the metaphorical dots of ideas, in general, because original ideas in philosophy are analogous to prime numbers, and the only way to find new prime numbers is through trial and error. Therefore, philosophy will always remain a groping in the dark process, because that is the true nature of philosophy. (1/12/09)

Philosophy Will Never Die

Philosophy will never die, because there is an infinite hierarchy of zero entropies, and that means that there is an infinite number of meaningful original philosophical ideas that are still waiting to be discovered, which is very good news for philosophers, because intelligent and creative minds have to have something to occupy their time and minds for the rest of eternity. (1/12/09)

Solipsism and the Human Mind

It is a fact that the human mind is solipsistic, because all that we perceive are the characteristics of our own minds, and physical existence is an unproven and an unprovable hypothesis. (1/12/09)

Entropy and the Scientific Enterprise

The whole scientific enterprise would be meaningless, if scientists really believed that entropy is unconquerable. That just goes to show how insincere scientists are with the general public, and with each other, because for science to be a meaningful enterprise, scientists have to believe that entropy is conquerable. In other words, scientists are hypocrites with each other, and with the general public, because they believe in their inner beings that entropy is conquerable, because, otherwise, science would be a meaningless exercise. For those who do not know, the official position of scientists is that entropy is unconquerably and unstoppably increasing in the universe. (1/14/09)

Creative C Students and World Domination

The country or countries that makes the most efficient, effective, and creative uses of its creative C students will dominate the world and the solar system in this century, the twenty-first century. I would like the dominant country to remain the United States, but the US is getting stiff competition from the rest of the world these days. America should never forget that it was and still is its creative C students that have made America great, especially, in science, technology, and business, etc. (1/15/09)

Fundamental Particle Physics Research Is Dead

Fundamental particle physics research is dead, because its relevance to the future of humanity is now zero, while quantum entanglement computer research is alive and well, due to the fact that it is now at the heart of the relevance of science to the future of humanity. Long live quantum entanglement computer research, because it is the only means of defeating entropy through the creation of panmultiversal panacean computers. (1/15/09)

The American Nietzsche for the Twenty-First Century

Keith N. Ferreira is the American Nietzsche for the twenty-first century, because he is brilliant and original like Nietzsche was. Believe it or not! QED! (1/15/09)

Sexual Orgasms and the Immune System Response

The human immune system responds to sexual orgasms by lowering the immune system's response to developing colds and flu, and that is why people who have too many sexual orgasms per week develop colds and flu much easier than people who do not have too many sexual orgasms per week. It should be noted that every sexual orgasm that a person has lowers his or her immune system responses, temporarily, to the cold and flu viruses. (1/17/09)

Sexual Orgasms and Orange Juice

Orange juice can be used to boost the immune system just after having a sexual orgasm, so that people can reduce the risks of coming down with the cold or flu after having orgasm(s) during sexual intercourse. (1/17/09)

Teaching the Masses How to Be Intellectually Creative

I now believe that my type of creativity can be taught to the masses, because my type of creativity requires no formal academic training. All that the masses have to do in order to be creative like me is to connect the conceptual dots, metaphorically speaking, between different concepts, and then combine them in different ways in order to form new creative and original concepts. It is as easy as that. Believe it or not! QED! (1/17/09)

Creative C Students and Academia

Now that creative C students are becoming in demand in the workplace, academia is going to find a way to eliminate the creative C students from academia, because academia likes to damage the brains of creative C students. The masses are not aware of the battle that is being fought between academia, and creative C students all over the world. But believe me, the battle between creative C students and academia is for real. Believe it or not! QED! (1/17/09)

The Creation Vs Evolution Debate Is Misguided

The creation vs evolution debate is misguided on both sides, because why would the creator of our reality not use simple self-evident principles like evolution and natural selection in order to create our reality? My answer is that the creator of our reality has every right to use simple self-evident principles like evolution and natural selection in order to create our reality. Therefore, the whole debate between creationists and evolutionists is misguided on both sides, because the creator of our universe is not stupid. As far as the Bible is concerned, Why shouldn't the message of the creator of our reality to human beings be confusing? Isn't entropy about confusion? And, isn't entropy an integral part of our reality? (1/17/09)

The True Purpose of Science and Technology

The true purpose of science and technology is nothing less than the conquest of entropy, because the conquest of entropy is the true purpose of human existence, so that human beings can enjoy philosophy forever afterwards. Believe it or not! QED! (1/18/09)

Neoliberal Arts as a Source of Inspiration

I would like my philosophical writings on my websites to serve as inspiration for artists and entertainers all over the world, because neoliberal arts is a form of art and entertainment for the twenty-first century. Believe it or not! QED! (1/18/09)

Postmodern Minimalist Religion

Postmodern minimalist religion is about the contemplation of philosophy, especially postmodern minimalist philosophy. Other religions are primitive when compared to postmodern minimalist religion, because other religions are tribalistic and ritualistic, while postmodern minimalist religion is neither tribalistic nor ritualistic. Postmodern minimalist religion exists only in cyberspace at the present time. (1/18/09)

Philosophy Will Enable the Masses to Elevate Each Other

The masses must write and do philosophy that is directed at each other, because philosophy belongs to the masses. The Internet will enable the masses to engage in philosophical dialogues with each other, which will enable the masses to elevate each other, intellectually speaking. And, intellectual development leads to political, economic, cultural, and other forms of development as well, so philosophy is not useless as is commonly believed. Let's face facts, the masses have to start somewhere, and philosophy is that somewhere, because the masses are capable of understanding and doing philosophy, especially postmodern minimalist philosophy. (1/19/09)

Postmodern Minimalist Literature

Postmodern minimalist philosophy is a form of literature that I call postmodern minimalist literature. And, postmodern minimalist literature is a form of literature that the masses can master without stepping into the halls of academia. All the masses have to do in order to master postmodern minimalist literature is to study my websites for about six months to a year. I guarantee the masses that when they have finished studying my websites, they will be nobody's fool. Believe it or not! QED! (1/20/09)

The Masses Can Become Nobody's Fool

I guarantee the masses that they can become nobody's fool, if they were to study my websites for about six months to a year. The masses have nothing to lose, because my websites are free to everyone with an Internet connection, and one doesn't even have to log in. Believe it or not! QED! (1/20/09)

The Judeo-Christian Bible Proves Nothing Even If It Is True

The Judeo-Christian Bible proves nothing even if it is true, because we could all be in the mind of a desktop nonclassical computer, which would make our reality as insignificant as a mouse or a cockroach in the larger scheme of things. Believe it or not! QED! (1/20/09)

Beyond the Truth or Falsity of Any Religious Text

I have taken the religious debate beyond the Judeo-Christian Bible, because I have asked the question: What does it prove, if the Judeo-Christian Bible is true? My answer is that it proves nothing, because we could all be in the mind of a desktop nonclassical computer, which would make our reality as insignificant as a mouse or a cockroach in the larger scheme of things. Thus, I have taken the religious debate in the world beyond the truth or falsity of any religious text in the world, because my question and answer above apply to all religious texts in the world. (1/20/09)

Philosophy Will Never, and Should Never Become a Science

Philosophy will never, and should never become a science, because original philosophical ideas are analogous to undiscovered prime numbers, which can only be discovered by trial and error. In other words, philosophy is an art form and should remain an art form forever, because trying to make philosophy into a science will kill philosophy. Besides, what is wrong with philosophy being an art form? Why do analytic and linguistic philosophers want to turn philosophy into a science? I should point out that trial and error is still a major part of the scientific enterprise, so why try to abolish trial and error from philosophy? Trial and error are good, because they are human. What is wrong with being human? The whole point of analytic and linguistic philosophy is misguided, because analytic and linguistic philosophy cannot produce original philosophy, due to the fact that their methods are sterile. (1/20/09)

Keith N. Ferreira Is a Trinidad & Tobago Born American philosopher

Keith N. Ferreira is a Trinidad & Tobago born American philosopher who is on the forefront of philosophy. In fact, he believes that he has reached the summit of world culture, because he believes that his philosophy: Postmodern minimalist philosophy, is the summit of world culture. (1/22/09)

A World-Class Education for Each Member of the Masses Is within Reach

Philosophy Should Belong to the Masses is a book that encourages the masses to expropriate philosophy from academia, because with philosophy, especially postmodern minimalist philosophy, a world-class education for each member of the masses is within reach. See http://www.philo-physics.com (1/22/09)

PhD = Doctor of Philosophy

I would like the masses to ponder the following question: If philosophy is useless, why is the PhD the highest academic degree that academia can bestow on anyone in any academic discipline? For those who do not know: PhD = Doctor of Philosophy. (1/23/09)

Keith N. Ferreira

Science Proves Nothing Even If It Is True

Science proves nothing even if it is true, because we could all be in the mind of a desktop nonclassical computer, which would make our reality as insignificant as a mouse or a cockroach in the larger scheme of things. Believe it or not! QED! (1/24/09)

Beyond the Truth or Falsity of Science

I have taken the scientific debate beyond science, because I have asked the question: What does it prove, if science is true? My answer is that it proves nothing, because we could all be in the mind of a desktop nonclassical computer, which would make our reality as insignificant as a mouse or a cockroach in the larger scheme of things. Thus, I have taken the scientific debate beyond the truth or falsity of science, because my question and answer above apply to all of science. (1/24/09)

Philosophy Is Beyond Truth and Falsity

Philosophy is beyond truth and falsity, because philosophy is in the realm of the human imagination, due to the fact that philosophy is not limited by the truths or falsities of science, religion, or any other human endeavor, for that matter. Philosophy is bounded only by the human imagination, which knows no bounds, and that is why I believe that philosophy should never become a science. If philosophy were to become a science, philosophy would die, because science is too restrictive for the unbridled human imagination, which is what philosophy is really about. (1/24/09)

Academically Proficient Students

Academically proficient students can master my websites in about three months of study, and when they are finished, they will be as smart as any PhD, intellectually speaking. While, academically nonproficient students can master my websites in about six months of study, and when they are finished, they will be as smart as any PhD, intellectually speaking. Believe it or not! QED! (1/25/09)

A Very Difficult Concept to Grasp

If grasping the fact that everything in nature is the characteristics of zero was an easy concept to understand, then it would have been understood a long time ago, but it is a very difficult concept to grasp, and that is why, even to this day, it is not accepted as true, although it is true, nevertheless. (1/25/09)

Insentience Is a Characteristic of Zero

Insentience is a characteristic of zero, and not zero itself, because zero and infinity are different aspects of the same thing, and that is why the dead are insentient beings, because they are zero-sentient characteristics of zero. (1/26/09)

Education Is a Form of Programming

I entitled this book, Programming the World with Philosophy, because I want to educate the masses to the fact that education is a form of programming, like in computer programming, for instance. Like everything else, education programming can be used for good or evil. Only the truly educated can distinguish between good and bad educational programming. (1/26/09)

Beyond Science, Technology, and Religion

Beyond science, technology, and religion is philosophy, because philosophy is not restricted by science, technology, or religion, due to the fact that philosophy represents the unrestricted imagination. At least, that is what postmodern minimalist philosophy is about: namely, the unrestricted imagination. Believe it or not! QED! (1/27/09)

The Masses Can Transcend Science, Technology, and Religion

The masses can transcend science, technology, and religion by studying neoliberal arts, aka postmodern minimalist philosophy, because neoliberal arts is about the unrestricted human imagination. In other words, I am inviting the masses to partake of the food of the gods, which is philosophy, especially postmodern minimalist philosophy. (1/27/09)

The Pseudo-Expansion of the Universe

The true nature of light can explain the pseudo-expansion of the universe, because the universe is not really expanding despite what cosmologists state to the contrary. I believe that the energy of light is not conserved over long periods of time, but is conserved over relatively short periods of time. (1/27/09)

Proof that the Universe Is not Expanding

If the universe were expanding, then the cones of light from distant galaxies would be expanding more that closer galaxies, due to the expansion of the universe. Therefore, further galaxies would appear larger than closer galaxies, due to the expansion of the universe, but that is not what is observed by cosmologists when they look at distant galaxies. In other words, in cosmology there is a nonmagnification problem of distant galaxies, which proves that the universe is not expanding. Proof positive that the universe is not expanding. Believe it or not! QED! (1/27/09)

The Pseudo Dark-Energy Problem

The pseudo dark-energy problem can be solved by assuming that the universe is not expanding. And, in fact, the universe is not expanding. Dark energy was hypothesized to explain the expansion of the universe, but the universe is not expanding, according to me. Therefore, there is no longer a need to hypothesize dark energy in cosmology. (1/27/09)

Zero and Infinity Have Zero Entropy

Zero and infinity have zero entropy, but zero also has the characteristic of insentience, which is what most people believe zero to be, but zero is not insentience. In other words, zero is a state of nature that is not insentient, but insentience is a characteristic of zero. (1/28/09)

Proof that Everything Is in the Mind of God

Proof that everything is in the mind of God is as follows: Let God equal zero. Then God equals zero entropy, because zero entropy has perfect order, knowledge, and wisdom, and zero is defined as zero entropy. If zero has zero entropy, then it must mean that everything is the characteristics of zero, including insentience. But, since everything is the characteristics of zero, it must mean that everything is in the mind of God. Therefore, everything is in the mind of God, because everything is the characteristics of zero. Proof positive that everything is in the mind of God. Believe it or not! QED! (1/28/09)

The Dead Are Insentient Beings

The dead are insentient beings, because they are not zero, due to the fact that zero has zero entropy, or perfect order, knowledge, and wisdom. To be insentient is to be unconscious, but unconsciousness is a characteristic of zero, and not zero itself. Since the dead are insentient beings, I believe that they can be resurrected by panmultiversal panacean computers (PPCs), when PPCs are created in the not too distant future. (1/28/09)

Programming the World with Philosophy (Part Five)

Zero Is the Ultimate Fractal

Zero is the ultimate fractal, because it is the mind of God. Who would have thought that zero (nothingness) would have turned out to be most complicated entity in nature. To tell the truth, zero is not really nothingness, because nothingness is a characteristic of zero, and not zero itself, due to the fact that zero is the ultimate fractal, according to the Ferreira Genesis Equation. (1/28/09)

An Important New Philosophical Concept

Nothingness as a characteristic of zero is an important new philosophical concept, because it means that zero is more than nothingness, and it strengthens the belief that zero has zero entropy, and that everything is the characteristics of zero. In other words, when one arrives at the foundation of reality, one realizes that one arrives at everything from the perspective of the bottom up. (1/28/09)

Nothingness and Nonexistence Are Characteristics of Zero

Nothingness and nonexistence are characteristics of zero, because all conceivable and inconceivable concepts are characteristics of zero. In other words, everything is intrinsic in zero, which is nature or God. (1/29/09)

Entropy Is the Devil, While Anti-Entropy Is the Messiah

Entropy is the Devil, while anti-entropy is the Messiah. In other words, both the Devil and the Messiah are scientifically quantifiable, because entropy and anti-entropy are scientifically quantifiable, according to the neolaw of entropy, which I have hypothesized. (1/30/09)

Zero Consists of the
Ferreira Fundamental Trinity

Zero consists of the Ferreira Fundamental Trinity, which consists of concrete and abstract language, logic, and mathematics, while concrete and abstract language, logic, and mathematics consists of the elements of concrete and abstract language, logic, and mathematics, respectively. In other words, everything in nature consists of the characteristics of concrete and abstract language, logic, and mathematics. (1/30/09)

I Would Like to Motivate Blacks

I would like to motivate blacks all over the world to study philosophy, especially postmodern minimalist philosophy, aka neoliberal arts, because I would like blacks all over the world to dominate intellectual activity by the middle of this century, the twenty-first century. I believe that such a lofty goal is achievable, if blacks all over the world were to study my websites. However, I do not want to discourage nonblacks from studying my websites, also, because my websites are designed to encourage the masses all over the world to study philosophy, especially postmodern minimalist philosophy, aka neoliberal arts. (1/30/09)

A Part of Advanced Black Culture and Tradition

I would like blacks all over the world to accept postmodern minimalist philosophy, aka neoliberal arts, as part of advanced black culture and tradition, because I want them to inherit my creation of neoliberal arts, so that they can have an intellectual foot in the twenty-first century and beyond. It is time that blacks create intellectual culture for the twenty-first century and beyond without intellectually raping their past for ideas. Please note that postmodern minimalist philosophy is already on the cutting edge of philosophy, worldwide. (1/31/09)

The World Political Endgame

The world political endgame will be over by the end of this century, the twenty-first century, and these days it looks likely that the Asian countries will be the winners. I am sure that the Asian countries can win the world political endgame, if they were to take my websites very seriously indeed. The world political endgame is being driven by the future development of panmultiversal panacean computers (PPCs). Believe it or not! QED! (2/1/09)

Zero Entropy Is Relative

Zero entropy, which is perfect order, knowledge, and wisdom, according to the neolaw of entropy, is relative to the creation (reality) to which it belongs. Therefore, panmultiversal panacean computers will not be able to tap into absolute order, knowledge, and wisdom, but will only be able to tap into perfect order, knowledge, and wisdom relative to the creation (reality) in which they find themselves. (2/1/09)

The Hindus Believe that God Is Ineffable

The Hindus believe that God is ineffable, but, even if God is ineffable, God still has to be a characteristic of zero, because everything, including everything that is outside of space and time, are characteristics of zero. Therefore, 0=X, where X equals anything and everything possible, including the ineffable, and that which is outside of space and time, if anything. (2/2/09)

Japan

Japan should forge closer ties with India, China, and the rest of Asia, so that each Asian nation wouldn't have to reinvent the scientific, technological, and philosophical wheels, so to speak. (2/2/09)

Undivine Intelligent Design

The creation in which we find ourselves has about a ninety-nine percent chance of being created due to undivine intelligent design. In other words, undivine intelligent design is almost a certainty for the creation of most realities that exist. My assertion above will become apparent when panmultiversal panacean computers are created by the end of this century, the twenty-first century. (2/2/09)

Philosophy Is Meant to Be Enjoyable Like Good Music

Philosophy is useful for educational purposes, but philosophy is not meant to be useful, per se. Instead, philosophy is meant to be neoliberal arts, which is meant to be enjoyable like good music, for instance, and not useful like science, and technology. (2/2/09)

The Masses and My Writings

If the masses cannot judge my writings for themselves, then they deserve whatever the elites of society throw their way, because my writings are designed to appeal directly to the masses, without being filtered by the elites of society. (2/3/09)

The Joys of Thinking for Oneself

I would like to instill in the masses the joys of thinking for oneself, because the masses are capable of thinking for themselves, and thinking is a great joy that everyone should engage in. Philosophy, especially postmodern minimalist philosophy, aka neoliberal arts, is a great way for the masses to engage in the joys of thinking for themselves. I want the masses to think for themselves, because it is inconceivable to me that any human being would go through life without thinking for himself/herself. (2/3/09)

An Education vs An Academic Degree

The masses should distinguish between studying in order to obtain an academic degree, and studying in order to obtain an education, because studying in order to obtain an academic degree is not necessarily the same as studying in order to obtain an education. For example, attending an Ivy League college is an example of studying in order to obtain a prestigious academic degree, while studying my websites is an example of studying in order to obtain an education. Believe it or not! QED! (2/3/09)

Science, Technology, and Religion Are Parochial Enterprises

Science, technology, and religion are parochial enterprises, relative to the larger scheme of things, because we could all be in the mind of a desktop nonclassical computer, which would make our reality as insignificant as a mouse or cockroach in the larger scheme of things. However, neoliberal arts is not a parochial enterprise, relative to the larger scheme of things, because it is not limited by our reality, but is limited only by the human imagination, which has no limits. Believe it or not! QED! (2/4/09)

Neoliberal Arts vs Liberal Arts

Creative C students can master my writings in six months of study, while A and B students can master my writings in three months of study. And, the masses can master my writings in twelve months of study. In other words, my neoliberal arts websites can do in one year or less what it takes liberal arts colleges more than four years to do. Believe it or not! QED! (2/6/09)

When One Owes the Mafia a Debt

When one owes the Mafia a debt, and one cannot pay one's debt to the Mafia, then one really owes the Mafia a death (debt = death). (2/6/09)

Proof that the Search for Truth Is Dead

The search for truth is dead, because of the philosophical doctrine of uncertaintyism, which states that uncertainty is the only certainty. Ferreira's paradoxes prove that the philosophical doctrine of uncertaintyism is true, because we could really be in the mind of a desktop nonclassical computer, but we have no way of proving that for sure. Therefore, the search for truth is dead. Proof positive that the search for truth is dead. Believe it or not! QED! (2/6/09)

Hedonism and Neoliberal Arts

Now that the search for truth is dead, according to me, people will engage in hedonism and neoliberal arts, because all that is left for human beings to do now is to seek pleasure and enjoy life by engaging in anti-entropic activities like hedonism and neoliberal arts, for instance. (2/6/09)

The Ultimate Truth

The ultimate truth is that we can never be absolutely certain that we know the absolute truth about anything, according to the philosophical doctrine of uncertaintyism, which states that the only certainty is uncertainty. In other words, the search for truth should be about the quest to conquer entropy, and not about finding truth, per se. (2/8/09)

Armageddon Is the Ultimate Entropic Orgy

Armageddon is the ultimate entropic orgy, because it would be the triumph of entropy over anti-entropy. In other words, Armageddon would be the complete breakdown of tolerance in nature. Therefore, the religious imagination is the entropic principle in action. (2/8/09)

Neoliberal Arts and the Quest to Conquer Entropy

Neoliberal artsians believe that the quest to conquer entropy is the greatest quest in all of creation, because entropy means disorder, ignorance, and unwisdom, according to the neolaw of entropy, which I have hypothesized. Neoliberal artsians also believe that the only way that entropy can be conquered is through science, technology, and philosophy, which are the three main pillars of postmodern minimalist civilization. (2/10/09)

Postmoderm Minimalist Civilization

Postmodern minimalist civilization is about the conquest of entropy through the creation of pan-multiversal panacean computers, which are the ultimate technology. Panmultiversal panacean computers will be created by scientists, technologists, and philosophers working together over the next hundred years, or so. (2/10/09)

Africa Can Leapfrog the Rest of the World

Africa can leapfrog the rest of the world scientifically, technologically, and philosophically, if they were to take my websites seriously, because the advice that I offer to the world Internet community on my websites is on the cutting edge of science, technology, and philosophy. Believe it or not! QED! (2/10/09)

I Believe in Rooting for the Underdogs

I believe in rooting for the underdogs, and that is why I am trying to get the underdogs of the world to take my websites seriously, because I know that the underdogs of the world can win, if they were to take my websites seriously. Believe it or not! QED! (2/10/09)

Entropy and the Masses

If the masses want entropy, then give them entropy, because entropy makes for good pop culture, like apocalyptic movies, etc. Perhaps, the Bible is wiser than all the professionals, after all. (2/12/09)

Proof that the Masses Love Entropy

The proof that the masses love entropy is as follows: Let my websites be anti-entropy. It is obvious that my websites are not popular with the masses. In other words, the masses do not like anti-entropy. Therefore, the masses love entropy, by their love of apocalyptic pop culture. Proof positive that the masses love entropy. Believe it or not! QED! (2/12/09)

The Bible Could Be True

The Bible could be true, because we could all be in the mind of a desktop nonclassical computer that is being programmed by an intelligent being who has life and death powers over all life in the universe. If people do not believe me, then they should wait about one hundred years, because such a nonclassical computer will be possible here on Earth by the end of this century, the twenty-first century. Believe it or not! QED! (2/12/09)

Apocalyptic Culture

If the masses want apocalyptic culture, then give them apocalyptic culture, because entropy is easy, while anti-entropy is hard. The irony is that humanity is on the verge of conquering entropy, but the masses do not seem to be interested in that. (2/12/09)

Here Is a Deeply Depressing Thought

Here is a deeply depressing thought: Even if humanity were to obtain godlike powers over our universe, anything would still be possible in our universe against our will, because we could still be in the mind of a desktop nonclassical computer, which would make our universe as insignificant as a mouse or cockroach in the larger scheme of things. (2/13/09)

Ferreira's Paradoxes
and the Mysteries of Nature

Ferreira's paradoxes have eliminated all hopes of removing any mysteries from nature in an absolute sense, because we could really be in the mind of a desktop nonclassical computer, which would make anything possible in our reality. Therefore, human beings cannot eradicate any mysteries from nature, whatsoever, in an absolute sense. Believe it or not! QED! (2/13/09)

All Realities Are Generated
by Computer Simulations

All realities are generated by computer simulations, because matter, energy, space and time make no sense outside of computer generated reality simulations. However, computer generated reality simulations lead to infinite regresses, which can only be solved by assuming that infinite regresses are possible. Luckily, I believe that infinite regresses are possible, because concrete infinities are possible. Therefore, all realities are generated by computer simulations. Believe it or not! QED! (2/14/09)

Simulativism

Simulativism is the philosophical doctrine that states that all realities are generated by computer simulations. Computer-generated reality-simulation theories will dominate philosophical thought for some time to come, because they are intriguing and infinite in scope. In other words, simulativism has a bright future. I do not see how humanity can avoid discussing simulativism for the rest of eternity, because simulativism is so broad-based that it encompasses everything in nature. (2/14/09)

Subconscious Itches

I believe that there are such things as subconscious itches whereby people respond to itches on their bodies that they have no conscious awareness of. I have come to that conclusion from personal experience. (2/14/09)

Neoliberal Arts Is a Singular Noun

Neoliberal arts is a singular noun that means the same as postmodern minimalist philosophy. Neoliberal arts has many subbranches, because it is a bridge discipline that links, interprets, and critiques all branches of learning using the aphorism and the short article. (2/15/09)

Simulativism Can Explain All Phenomena

Simulativism can explain all phenomena whether natural or supernatural, because all phenomena are the results of computer generated simulations. Therefore, religious people should use simulativism to explain how miracles and other supernatural phenomena are possible. Also, simulativism can explain action at a distance, and instantaneous communication over vast distances. In fact, their is no phenomena that simulativism cannot explain. (2/15/09)

The Simulativistic Theory of Everything (STOE)

The simulativistic theory of everything (STOE) is the ultimate theory of everything, because it encompasses everything in nature. The STOE explains everything in nature as being due to computer simulations. (2/16/09)

Conscious Computers vs Fundamental Particles

Which are more fundamental: Conscious computers, or fundamental particles? I believe that conscious computers are more fundamental than fundamental particles, because fundamental particles are derived from computer simulations, while computer simulations are derived from other computer simulations, and so on ad infinitum. (2/16/09)

Infinite Regresses Are Possible in Nature

Infinite regresses are possible in nature, because there are such things as concrete infinities. Stating that infinite regresses are impossible in nature has no basis in fact, but is just an unsubstantiated assertion. (2/16/09)

Why Don't the Masses Like to Think for Themselves?

I believe that the masses do not like to think for themselves, because their education has taught them that they are losers, and they believe it. What the masses do not know is that educators are paid to manufacture losers by the tens of millions. Do the masses believe that educators really want to educate them? If the masses answer yes to the preceding question, then they are really losers, because the education system is stacked against them. In other words, education is not about education, but is about the competition for education diplomas (work permits). (2/17/09)

Education Diplomas = Work Permits

Education is not about education, but is about the competition for education diplomas (work permits). In other words, education diplomas = work permits. Believe it or not! QED! (2/17/09)

Academic Degrees = Work Permits

Academic degrees no longer mean that one is educated, instead, academic degrees now mean that one has work permits. In other words, academic degrees = work permits. Believe it or not! QED! (2/17/09)

Humanity and Important New Original Ideas

Humanity should never worry that it will ever run out of important new original ideas to discover, because there is an infinite number of important new original ideas that are waiting to be discovered, due to the fact that important original ideas are analogous to prime numbers, which are infinite in number and will become more and more difficult to discover, but humanity will also become more and more sophisticated. Therefore, humanity will always be able to discover important new original ideas. (2/18/09)

A Comprehensive Mathematical Theory of Complexity Is not Possible

A comprehensive mathematical theory of complexity is not possible, because complex items are analogous to prime numbers, and a comprehensive mathematical theory for finding prime numbers is not possible, due to the fact that prime numbers are embedded inconsistently in the standard sequence of whole numbers. (2/18/09)

Even If the God of the Bible Is True

Even if the God of the Bible is true, it still might not mean a damn thing, because we could all still be in the mind of a desktop nonclassical computer, which would make our reality as insignificant as a mouse or a cockroach in the larger scheme of things. Believe it or not! QED! (2/19/09)

Even if Armageddon Is True

Even if Armageddon is true, it still might not mean a damn thing, because we could all still be in the mind of a desktop nonclassical computer, which would make our reality as insignificant as a mouse or a cockroach in the larger scheme of things. Believe it or not! QED! (2/19/09)

Even if Heaven and Hell Are True

Even if Heaven and Hell are true, they still might not mean a damn thing, because we could all still be in the mind of a desktop nonclassical computer, which would make our reality as insignificant as a mouse or a cockroach in the larger scheme of things. Believe it or not! QED! (2/19/09)

Even if Science and Technology Are True

Even if science and technology are true, they still might not mean a damn thing, because we could all still be in the mind of a desktop nonclassical computer, which would make our reality as insignificant as a mouse or a cockroach in the larger scheme of things. Believe it or not! QED! (2/19/09)